I0673666

Benjamin Palmer

Slavery - A Divine Trust

The Duty of the South to Preserve and Perpetuate the Institution as it Now

Exists

Benjamin Palmer

Slavery - A Divine Trust
The Duty of the South to Preserve and Perpetuate the Institution as it Now Exists

ISBN/EAN: 9783337361709

Printed in Europe, USA, Canada, Australia, Japan

Cover: Foto ©Andreas Hilbeck / pixelio.de

More available books at **www.hansebooks.com**

SLAVERY

A

DIVINE TRUST.

THE DUTY OF THE SOUTH

TO

PRESERVE AND PERPETUATE THE INSTITUTION

AS IT NOW EXISTS.

NEW-YORK:

GEORGE F. NESBITT & CO., PRINTERS,

CORNER OF PEARL AND PINE STREETS,

1861.

transmit our existing system of domestic servitude, with the right, un-changed by man, to go and root itself wherever Providence and nature may carry it."—DR. PALMER.

THANKSGIVING SERMON,

DELIVERED AT THE

First Presbyterian Church, New Orleans,

On Thursday, December 29, 1860,

BY

REV. B. M. PALMER, D. D.

———•—•———

.

NEW-YORK:
GEORGE F. NESBITT & CO., PRINTERS,
CORNER OF PEARL AND PINE STS.

1861.

[From the *Sunday Delta*, New Orleans]

SERMON.

———•◄♦►•———

Shall the throne of iniquity have fellowship with thee, which frameth mischief by a law ?—PSALM xciv, 20.

All the men of thy confederacy have brought thee even to the border ; the men that were at peace with thee have deceived thee, and prevailed against thee ; they that ate thy bread have laid a wound under thee ; there is none understanding in him.—OBADIAH v.

The voice of the Chief Magistrate has summoned us to-day to the house of prayer. This call, in its annual repetition, may be, too often, only a solemn state-form ; nevertheless, it covers a mighty and a double truth.

It recognizes the existence of a personal God, whose will shapes the destiny of nations, and that sentiment of religion in man which points to Him as the needle to the pole. Even with those who grope in the twilight of natural religion, natural conscience gives a voice to the dispensations of Providence. If in autumn " extensive harvests hang their heavy head," the joyous reaper, " crowned with the sickle and the wheaten sheaf," lifts his heart to the "Father of lights, from whom cometh down every good and perfect gift." Or, if pestilence and famine waste the earth, even pagan altars smoke with bleeding victims, and costly hecatombs appease the divine anger which flames out in such dire misfortunes. It is the instinct of man's religious nature, which, among Christians and heathens alike, seeks after God—the natural homage which reason, blinded as it may be, pays to a universal and ruling Providence. All classes bow beneath its spell, especially in seasons of gloom, when a nation bends beneath the weight of a general calamity, and a common sorrow falls upon . every heart. The hesitating skeptic forgets to weigh his scruples, as the dark shadow passes over him and fills his soul with awe.

The dainty philosopher, coolly discoursing of the forces of nature and her uniform laws, abandons for a time his atheistical speculations, abashed by the proofs of a supreme and personal will.

Thus the devout followers of Jesus Christ, and those who do not rise above the level of mere theism, are drawn into momentary fellowship; as, under the pressure of these inextinguishable convictions, they pay a public and united homage to the God of nature and grace.

In obedience to this great law of religious feeling, not less than in obedience to the civil ruler who represents this Commonwealth in its unity, we are now assembled. Hitherto, on similar occasions, our language has been the language of gratitude and song. "The voice of rejoicing and salvation was in the tabernacles of the righteous." Together we praised the Lord "that our garners were full, affording all manner of store; that our sheep brought forth thousands and tens of thousands in our streets; that our oxen were strong to labor, and there was no breaking in nor going out, and no complaining was in our streets." As we together surveyed the blessings of Providence, the joyful chorus swelled from millions of people, "Peace be within thy walls, and prosperity within thy palaces." But, to-day, burdened hearts all over this land are brought to the sanctuary of God. We "see the tents of Cushan in affliction, and the curtains of the land of Midian do tremble." We have fallen upon times when there are "signs in the sun, and in the moon, and in the stars; upon the earth distress of nations, with perplexity; the sea and the waves roaring; men's hearts failing them for fear, and for looking after those things which are coming " in the near, yet gloomy, future. Since the words of this proclamation were penned by which we are convened, that which all men dreaded, but against which all men hoped, has been realized; and in the triumph of a sectional majority, we are compelled to read the probable doom of our once happy and united confederacy. It is not to be concealed, that we —— in the most fearful and perilous crisis which has occurred in our history as a nation. The cords which, during four-fifths of a century, have bound together this growing Republic, are now strained to their utmost tension—they just need the touch of fire to part asunder forever. Like a ship laboring in the storm, and suddenly grounded upon some treacherous shoal, every timber of this vast confederacy strains and groans under the pressure. Sectional divisions, the jealousy of rival interests, the lust of political power, a bastard ambition, which looks to personal aggrandizement rather than to the public weal, a reckless radicalism, which seeks for the subversion of all that is ancient and stable, and a furious fanaticism, which drives on its ill-considered conclusions with utter disregard of the evil it engenders—all these combine to create a portentous crisis, the like of which we have never known before, and which puts to a crucifying test the virtue, the patriotism, and the piety of the country.

You, my hearers, who have waited upon my public ministry, and have known me in the intimacies of pastoral intercourse, will do me the justice to testify that I have never intermeddled with political questions. Interested as I might be in the progress of events, I have never obtruded, either publicly or privately, my opinions upon any of you ; nor can a single man arise and say that, by word or sign, have I ever sought to warp his sentiments or control his judgment upon any political subject whatsoever. The party questions which have hitherto divided the political world, have seemed to me to involve no issue sufficiently momentous to warrant my turning aside, even for a moment, from my chosen calling. In this day of intelligence, I have felt there were thousands around me more competent to instruct in statesmanship ; and thus, from considerations of modesty, no less than prudence, I have preferred to move among you as a preacher of righteousness belonging to a kingdom not of this world.

During the heated canvass which has just been brought to so disastrous a close, the seal of a rigid and religious silence has not been broken. I deplored the divisions amongst us, as being, to a large extent, impertinent in the solemn crisis which was too evidently impending. Most clearly did it appear to me that but one issue was before us ; an issue soon to be presented in a form which would compel the attention. That crisis might make it imperative upon me, as a Christian and a divine, to speak in language admitting no misconstruction. Until then, aside from the din and strife of parties, I could only mature, with solitary and prayerful thought, the destined utterance. That hour has come. At a juncture so solemn as the present, with the destiny of a great people waiting upon the decision of an hour, it is not lawful to be still. Whoever may have influence to shape public opinion, at such a time must lend it, or prove faithless to a trust as solemn as any to be accounted for at the bar of God.

Is it immodest in me to assume that I may represent a class whose opinions in such a controversy are of cardinal importance—the class which seeks to ascertain its duty in the light simply of conscience and religion, and which turns to the moralist and the Christian for support and guidance? The question, too, which now places us upon the brink of revolution, was, in its origin, a question of morals and religion. It was debated in ecclesiastical councils before it entered legislative halls. It has riven asunder the two largest religious communions in the land; and the right determination of this primary question will go far toward fixing the attitude we must assume in the coming struggle. I sincerely pray God that I may be forgiven if I have misapprehended the duty incumbent upon me to-day; for I have ascended this pulpit under the agitation of feeling natural to one who is about to deviate from the settled policy of his public life. It is my purpose—not as your organ, compromiting you, whose opinions are for the most part unknown to me, but on my sole responsibility—to speak upon the one question of the day; and to state the duty which, as I believe, patriotism and religion alike requires of us all. I shall aim to speak with a moderation of tone and feeling almost judicial, well befitting the sanctities of the place and the solemnities of the judgment-day.

In determining our duty in this emergency, it is necessary that we should first ascertain the nature of the trust providentially committed to us. A nation often has a character as well-defined and intense as that of the individual. This depends, of course, upon a variety of causes, operating through a long period of time. It is due largely to the original traits which distinguish the stock from which it springs, and to the providential training which has formed its education. But, however derived, this individuality of character alone makes any people truly historic, competent to work out its specific mission, and to become a factor in the world's progress. The particular trust assigned to such a people becomes the pledge of Divine protection, and their fidelity to it determines the fate by which it is finally overtaken. What that trust is must be ascertained from the necessities of their position, the institutions which are the outgrowth of their principles, and the conflicts through which they preserve their identity and independence. If, then, the South is such a people, what, at this juncture, is their providential trust? I answer, that it is *to conserve and to perpetuate the institution of domestic slavery as now existing.* It is not necessary here to inquire whether this is precisely the best relation in which the hewer of wood and drawer of water can stand to his employer; although this proposition may perhaps be successfully sustained by those who choose to defend it. Still less are we required, dogmatically, to affirm that it will subsist through all time. Baffled as our wisdom may now be, in finding a solution of this intricate social problem, it would, nevertheless, be the height of arrogance to pronounce what changes may or may not occur in the distant future. In the grand march of events, Providence may work out a solution undiscoverable by us. What modifications of soil and climate may hereafter be produced, what consequent changes in the products on which we depend, what political revolutions may occur among the races which are now enacting the great drama of history;—all such inquiries are totally irrelevant, because no prophetic vision can pierce the darkness of that future. If this question should ever arise, the generation to whom it is remitted will doubtless have the wisdom to meet it, and Providence will furnish the lights in which it is to be resolved. All that we claim for them and for ourselves is liberty to work out this problem, guided by nature and God, without obtrusive interference from abroad. These great questions of providence and history must have free scope for their solution; and the race whose fortunes are distinctly implicated in the same is alone authorized, as it is alone competent, to determine them. It is just this impertinence of human legislation, setting bounds to what God only can regulate, that the South is called this day to resent and resist. The country is convulsed simply because "the throne of iniquity frameth mischief by a law." Without, therefore, determining the question of duty for future generations, I simply say, that for us, as now situated, the duty is plain of conserving and transmitting the system of slavery, with the freest scope for its natural development and extension. Let us, my brethren, look our duty in the face. With this institution assigned to our keeping, what reply shall we make to those who say that its days are numbered? My own conviction is, that we should at once lift ourselves, intelligently, to the highest moral ground, and proclaim to all the world that we hold this trust from God, and in its occupancy we are prepared to stand or fall as God may appoint. If the critical moment has arrived at which the great issue is joined, let us say that, in the sight of all perils, we will stand by our trust: and God be with the right!

The argument which enforces the solemnity of this providential trust is simple and condensed. It is bound upon us, then, by the *principle of self-preservation*, that "first law" which is continually asserting its supremacy over others. Need I pause to show how this system of servitude underlies and supports our material interests? That our wealth consists in our lands, and in the serfs who till them? That from the nature of our products they can only be cultivated by labor which must be controlled in order to be certain? That any other than a tropical race must faint and wither beneath a tropical sun? Need I pause to show how this system is interwoven with our entire social fabric? That these slaves form parts of our households, even as our children; and that, too, through a relationship recognized and sanctioned in the scriptures of God even as the other? Must I pause to show how it has fashioned our modes of life, and determined all our habits of thought and feeling, and moulded the very type of our civilization? How, then, can the hand of violence be laid upon it without involving our existence? The so-called free States of this country are working out the social problem under conditions peculiar to themselves. These conditions are sufficiently hard, and their success is too uncertain, to excite in us the least jealousy of their lot. With a teeming population, which the soil cannot support—

with their wealth depending upon arts, created by artificial wants—
with an eternal friction between the grades of their society—with
their labor and their capital grinding against each other like the
upper and nether millstones—with labor cheapened and displaced
by new mechanical inventions, bursting more asunder the bonds
of brotherhood; amid these intricate perils we have ever given
them our sympathy and our prayers, and have never sought to
weaken the foundations of their social order. God grant them
complete success in the solution of all their perplexities! We,
too, have our responsibilities and our trials; but they are all bound
up in this one institution, which has been the object of such un-
righteous assault through five and twenty years. If we are true
to ourselves, we shall, at this critical juncture, stand by it, and work
out our destiny.

This duty is bound upon us again *as the constituted guardians of
the slaves themselves.* Our lot is not more implicated in theirs,
than is their lot in ours; in our mutual relations we survive or
perish together. The worst foes of the black race are those who
have intermeddled on their behalf. We know better than others
that every attribute of their character fits them for dependence
and servitude. By nature, the most affectionate and loyal of all
races beneath the sun, they are also the most helpless; and no
calamity can befall them greater than the loss of that protection
they enjoy under this patriarchal system. Indeed, the experiment
has been grandly tried of precipitating them upon freedom, which
they know not how to enjoy; and the dismal results are before
us, in statistics that astonish the world. With the fairest portions
of the earth in their possession, and with the advantage of a long
discipline as cultivators of the soil, their constitutional indolence
has converted the most beautiful islands of the sea into a howling
waste. It is not too much to say, that if the South should, at
this moment, surrender every slave, the wisdom of the entire world,
united in solemn council, could not solve the question of their dis-
posal. Their transportation to Africa, even if it were feasible,
would be but the most refined cruelty; they must perish with
starvation before they could have time to relapse into their prim-
itive barbarism. Their residence here, in the presence of the

2

vigorous Saxon race, would be but the signal for their rapid ex-
termination before they had-time to waste away through listless-
ness, filth and vice. Freedom would be their doom; and equally
from both they call upon us, their providential guardians, to be
protected. I know this argument will be scoffed abroad as the
hypocritical cover thrown over our own cupidity and selfishness;
but every Southern master knows its truth and feels its power.
My servant, whether born in my house or bought with my money,
stands to me in the relation of a child. Though providentially
owing me service, which, providentially, I am bound to exact, he
is, nevertheless, my brother and my friend; and I am to him a
guardian and a father. He leans upon me for protection, for
counsel, and for blessing; and so long as the relation continues,
no power, but the power of almighty God, shall come between
him and me. Were there no argument but this, it binds upon us
the providential duty of preserving the relation that we may save
him from a doom worse than death.

It is a duty which we owe, further, *to the civilized world.* It is
a remarkable fact, that during these thirty years of unceasing war-
fare against slavery, and while a lying spirit has inflamed the
world against us, that world has grown more and more dependent
upon it for sustenance and wealth. Every tyro knows that all
branches of industry fall back upon the soil. We must come,
every one of us, to the bosom' of this great mother for nourish-
ment. In the happy partnership which has grown up in providence between the tribes of this confederacy, our industry has
been concentrated upon agriculture. To the North we have
cheerfully resigned all the profits arising from manufacture and
commerce. Those profits they have, for the most part, fairly
earned, and we have never begrudged them. We have sent them
our sugar, and bought it back when refined; we have sent them
our cotton, and bought it back when spun into thread or woven
into cloth. Almost every article we use, from the shoe-latchet to
the most elaborate and costly article of luxury, they have made
and we have bought; and both sections have thriven by the partnership, as no people ever thrived before since the first shining of
the sun. So literally true are the words of the text, addressed by

Obadiah to Edom, "All the men of our confederacy, the men that were at peace with us, have eaten our bread-at the very time they have deceived and laid a wound under us." Even beyond this—the enriching commerce which has built the splendid cities and marble palaces of England as well as of America, has been largely established upon the products of our soil; and the blooms upon Southern fields, gathered by black hands, have fed the spindles and looms of Manchester and Birmingham not less than of Lawrence and Lowell. Strike now a blow at this system of labor, and the world itself totters at the stroke. Shall we permit that blow to fall? Do we not owe it to civilized man to stand in the breach and stay the uplifted arm? If the blind Samson lays hold of the pillars which support the arch of the world's industry, how many more will be buried beneath its ruins than the lords of the Philistines? "Who knoweth whether we are not come to the kingdom for such a time as this?"

Last of all, in this great struggle, *we defend the cause of God and religion.* The Abolition spirit is undeniably atheistic. The demon which erected its throne upon the guillotine in the days of Robespierre and Marat, which abolished the Sabbath, and worshiped reason in the person of a harlot, yet survives to work other horrors, of which those of the French revolution are but the type. Among a people so generally religious as the American, a disguise must be worn; but it is the same old threadbare disguise of the advocacy of human rights. From a thousand Jacobin clubs here, as in France, the decree has gone forth which strikes at God by striking at all subordination and law. Availing itself of the morbid and misdirected sympathies of men, it has entrapped weak consciences in the meshes of its treachery; and now, at last, has seated its high-priest upon the throne, clad in the black garments of discord and schism, so symbolic of its ends. Under this specious cry of reform, it demands that every evil shall be corrected, or society become a wreck—the sun must be stricken from the heavens, if a spot is found on his disk. The Most High, knowing his own power, which is infinite, and his own wisdom, which is unfathomable, can afford to be patient. But these self-constituted reformers must quicken the activity of Jehovah, or compel his abdication.

In their furious haste, they trample upon obligations sacred as any which can bind the conscience. It is time to reproduce the obsolete idea that Providence must govern man, and not that man should control Providence. In the imperfect state of human society, it pleases God to allow evils which check others that are greater. As in the physical world, objects are moved forward, not by a single force, but by the composition of forces; so in his moral administration, there are checks and balances whose intimate relations are comprehended only by himself. But what reck they of this—these fierce zealots who undertake to drive the chariot of the sun? working out the single and false idea which rides them like a nightmare, they dash athwart the spheres, utterly disregarding the delicate mechanism of Providence; which moves on wheels within wheels, with pivots, and balances, and springs, which the great designer alone can control. This spirit of atheism, which knows no God who tolerates evil, no Bible which sanctions law, and no conscience that can be bound by oaths and covenants, has selected us for its victims, and slavery for its issue. Its banner-cry rings out already upon the air—"Liberty, equality, fraternity," which, simply interpreted, mean bondage, confiscation and massacre. With its tricolor waving in the breeze, it waits to inaugurate its reign of terror. To the South the highest position is assigned, of defending, before all nations, the cause of all religion and of all truth. In this trust, we are resisting the power which wars against constitutions, and laws and compacts, against Sabbaths and sanctuaries, against the family, the State and the church; which blasphemously invades the prerogatives of God, and rebukes the Most High for the errors of his administration, which, if it cannot snatch the reins of empire from his grasp, will lay the universe in ruins at his feet. Is it possible that we shall decline the onset?

This argument, then, which sweeps over the entire circle of our relations, touches the four cardinal points of duty *to ourselves, to our slaves, to the world, and to almighty God.* It establishes the nature and solemnity of our present trust to *preserve and transmit our existing system of domestic servitude, with the right, unchanged by man, to go and root itself wherever Providence and nature may carry it.* This trust we will discharge in the face of the worst possible peril. Though war be the aggregation of all evils, yet, should the madness of the hour appeal to the arbitration of the sword, we will not shrink even from the baptism of fire. If modern crusa· ders stand in serried ranks upon some plain of Esdraelon, there shall we be in defense of our trust. Not till the last man has fallen behind the last rampart, shall it drop from our hands; and then only in surrender to the God who gave it.

Against this institution a system of aggression has been pursued through the last thirty years. Initiated by· a few fanatics, who were at first despised, it has gathered strength from opposition until it has assumed its present gigantic proportions. No man has thoughtfully watched the progress of this controversy without being convinced that the crisis must at length come. Some few, perhaps, have hoped against hope, that the gathering imposthume might be dispersed, and the poison be eliminated from the body politic by healthful remedies. But the delusion has scarcely been cherished by those who have studied the history of fanaticism, in its path of blood and fire through the ages of the past. The mo· ment must arrive when the conflict must be joined, and victory decide for one or the other. As it has been a war of legislative tactics, and not of physical force, both parties have been maneu· vering for a position; and the embarrassment has been, while dodging amidst constitutional forms, to make an issue that should be clear, simple and tangible, Such an issue is at length presented in the result of the recent Presidential election. Be it observed, too, that it is an issue made by the North, not by the South; upon whom, therefore, must rest the entire guilt of the present disturb· ance. With a choice between three national candidates, who have more or less divided the vote of the South, the North, with unex· ampled unanimity, have cast their ballot for a candidate who is sectional, who represents a party that is sectional, and the ground of that sectionalism, prejudiced against the established and consti· tutional rights and immunities and institutions of the South. What does this declare—what can it declare—but that from hence· forth this is to be a government of section over section; a govern· ment using constitutional forms only to embarrass and divide the section ruled, and as fortresses through whose embrasures the cannon of legislation is to be employed in demolishing the guaranteed institutions of the South? What issue is more direct, concrete, intelligible, than this? I thank God that, since the conflict must be joined, the responsibility of this issue rests not with us, who have ever acted upon the defensive; and that it is so disembarrassed and simple that the feeblest mind can understand it.

The question with the South to-day is not what issue shall *she* make, but how shall she meet that which is prepared for her? Is it possible that we can hesitate longer than a moment? In our natural recoil from the perils of revolution, and with our clinging fondness for the memories of the past, we may perhaps look around for something to soften the asperity of this issue, for some ground on which we may defer the day of evil, for some hope that the gathering clouds may not burst in fury upon the land.

It is alleged, for example, that the President elect has been chosen by a fair majority, under prescribed forms. But need I say, to those who have read history, that no despotism is more absolute than that of an unprincipled democracy, and no tyranny more galling than that exercised through constitutional formulas? But the plea is idle, when the very question we debate is the perpetuation of that constitution now converted into an engine of oppression, and the continuance of that union which is henceforth to be our condition of vassalage. I say it with solemnity and pain, this union of our forefathers is already gone. It existed but in mutual confidence, the bonds of which were ruptured in the late election. Though its form should be preserved, it is, in fact, destroyed. We may possibly entertain the project of reconstructing it; but it will be another union, resting upon other than past guarantees. "In that we say a new covenant, we have made the first old, and that which decayeth and waxeth old is ready to vanish away"—"as a vesture it is folded up." For myself, I say, that under the rule which threatens us, I throw off the yoke of this union as readily as did our ancestors the yoke of King George III., and for causes immeasurably stronger than those pleaded in their celebrated declaration.

It is softly whispered, too, that the successful competitor for the throne protests and avers his purpose to administer the government in a conservative and national spirit. Allowing him all credit for personal integrity in these protestations, he is, in this matter, nearly as impotent for good as he is competent for evil. He is nothing more than a figure upon the political chess-board—whether pawn, or knight, or king, will hereafter appear—but still a silent figure upon the checkered squares, moved by the hands of an unseen player. That player is the party to which he owes his elevation ; a party that has signalized its history by the most unblushing perjuries. What faith can be placed in the protestations of men who openly avow that their consciences are too sublimated to be restrained by the obligation of covenants or by the sanctity of oaths? No: we have seen the trail of the serpent five and twenty years in our Eden; twined now in the branches of the forbidden tree, we feel the pangs of death already begun, as its hot breath is upon our cheek, hissing out the original falsehood, " Ye shall not surely die."

Another suggests, that even yet the electors, alarmed by these demonstrations of the South, may not cast the black ball which dooms their country to the executioner. It is a forlorn hope. Whether we should counsel such breach of faith in them, or take refuge in their treachery—whether such a result would give a President chosen by the people according to the Constitution—are points I will not discuss. But that it would prove a cure for any of our ills, who can believe? It is certain that it would, with some show of justice, exasperate a party sufficiently ferocious—that it would doom us to four years of increasing strife and bitterness— and that the crisis must come at last, under issues possibly not half so clear as the present. Let us not desire to shift the day of trial by miserable subterfuges of this sort. The issue is upon us ; let us meet it like men, and end, this strife forever.

But some quietist whispers, yet further, this majority is accidental, and has been swelled by accessions of men simply opposed to the existing administration ; the party is utterly heterogeneous, and must be shivered into fragments by its own success. I confess, frankly, this suggestion has staggered me more than any other, and I sought to take refuge therein. Why should we not wait and see the effect of success itself upon a party whose elements might devour each other in the very distribution of the spoil? Two considerations have dissipated the fallacy before me. The first is, that, however mixed the party, Abolitionism is clearly its informing and actuating soul; and fanaticism is a blood-hound that never bolts its track when it has once lapped blood. The elevation of their candidate is far from being the consummation of their aims; it is only the beginning of that consummation; and, if all history be not a lie, there will be cohesion enough till the end of the beginning is reached, and the dreadful banquet of slaughter and ruin shall glut the appetite. The second consideration is a principle which I cannot blink. It is nowhere denied that the first article in the creed of the new dominant party is the restriction of slavery within its present limits. It is distinctly avowed by their organs, and in the name of their elected chieftain, as will appear from the following extract from an article written to pacify the South, and to reassure its fears:—

"There can be no doubt whatever in the mind of any man, that Mr. Lincoln regards slavery as a moral, social and political evil, and that it should be dealt with as such by the Federal Government, in every instance where it is called upon to deal with it at all. On this point there is no room for question—and there need be no misgivings as to his official action. The whole influence of the Executive Department of the Government, while in his hands, will be thrown against the extension of slavery into the new territories of the Union, and the reopening of the African slave trade. On these points he will make no compromise, nor yield one hair's breadth to coercion from any quarter or in any shape. He does not accede to the alleged decision of the Supreme Court, that the Constitution places slaves upon the footing of other property, and protects them as such wherever its jurisdiction extends; nor will he be, in the least degree, governed or controlled by it in his executive action. He will do all in his power, personally and officially, by the direct exercise of the powers of his office, and the indirect influence inseparable from it, to arrest the tendency to make slavery national and perpetual, and to place it in precisely the same position which it held in the early days of the Republic, and in the view of the founders of the Government."

Now, what enigmas may be couched in this last sentence, the sphinx which uttered them can perhaps resolve; but the sentence in which they occur is as big as the belly of the Trojan horse which laid the city of Priam in ruins.

These utterances we have heard so long, that they fall stale upon the ear; but never before have they had such significance. Hitherto they have come from Jacobin conventicles and pulpits, from the rostrum, from the hustings, and from the halls of our national Congress; but always as the utterances of irresponsible men, or associations of men. But now the voice comes from the throne; already, before clad with the sanctities of office, ere the anointing oil is poured upon the monarch's head, the decree has gone forth that the institution of Southern slavery shall be constrained within assigned limits. Though nature and Providence should send forth its branches like the banyan-tree, to take root in congenial soil, here is a power superior to both, that says it shall wither and die within its own charmed circle.

What say you to this, to whom this great providential trust of conserving slavery is assigned? "Shall the throne of iniquity have fellowship with thee which frameth mischief by a law?" It is this that makes the crisis. Whether we will or not, this is the historic moment when the fate of this institution hangs suspended in the balance. Decide either way, it is the moment of our destiny—the only thing affected by the decision is the complexion of that destiny. If the South bows before this throne, she accepts the decree of restriction and ultimate extinction, which is made the condition of her homage.

As it appears to me, the course to be pursned in this emergency is that which has already been inaugurated. Let the people in all the Southern States, in solemn counsel assembled, reclaim the powers they have delegated. Let those conventions be composed of men whose fidelity has been approved—men who bring the wisdom, experience and firmness of age to support and announce principles which have long been matured. Let these conventions decide firmly and solemnly what they will do with this great trust committed to their hands. Let them pledge each other, in sacred covenant, to uphold and perpetuate what they cannot resign without dishonor and palpable ruin. Let them, further, take all the necessary steps looking to separate and independent existence, and initiate measures for framing a new and homogeneous confederacy. Thus, prepared for every contingency, let the

3

crisis come. Paradoxical as it may seem, if there be any way to save, or rather to reconstruct, the union of our forefathers, it is this.

Perhaps, at the last moment, the conservative portions of the North may awake to see the abyss into which they are about to plunge. Perchance they may arise and crush out forever the Abolition hydra, and cast it into a grave from which there shall never be a resurrection.

Thus, with restored confidence, we may be rejoined a united and happy people. But, before God, I believe that nothing will effect this but the line of policy which the South has been compelled in self-preservation to adopt. I confess frankly I am not sanguine that such an auspicious result will be reached. Partly, because I do not see how new guarantees are to be grafted upon the constitution, nor how, if grafted, they can be more binding than those which have already been trampled under foot; but, chiefly, because I do not see how such guarantees can be elicited from the people at the North. It cannot be disguised that, almost to a man, they are antislavery where they are not Abolition. A whole generation has been educated to look upon the system with abhorrence as a national blot. They hope, and look, and pray for its extinction within a reasonable time, and, cannot be satisfied unless things are seen drawing to that conclusion. We, on the contrary, as its constituted guardian, can demand nothing less than that it should be left open to expansion, subject to no limitations, save those imposed by God and nature. I fear the antagonism is too great, and the conscience of both parties too deeply implicated, to allow such a composition of the strife. Nevertheless, since it is within the range of possibility in the providence of God, I would not shut out the alternative.

Should it fail, what remains but that we say to each other, calmly and kindly, what Abraham said to Lot: "Let there be no strife, I pray thee, between me and thee, and between my herdmen and thy herdmen, for we be brethren. Is not the whole land before thee? Separate thyself, I pray thee, from me—if thou wilt take the left hand, then I will go to the right, or if thou depart to the right hand, then I will go to the left." Thus, if we cannot

save the Union, we may save the inestimable blessings it en-
shrines ; if we cannot preserve the vase, we will preserve the pre-
cious liquor it contains.

In all this, I speak for the North no less than for the South ;
for on our united and determined resistance at this moment depends the salvation of the whole country—in saving ourselves we
shall save the North from the ruin she is madly drawing down
upon her own head.

The position of the South is at this moment sublime. If she
has grace given her to know her hour, she will save herself, the
country, and the world. It will involve, indeed, temporary pros-
tration and distress; the dikes of Holland must be cut to save
her from the troops of Philip. But I warn my countrymen, the
historic moment once passed, never returns. If she will arise in
her majesty, and speak now as with the voice of one man, she will
roll back for all time the curse that is upon her. If she succumbs
now, she transmits that curse as an heir-loom to posterity.

We may, for a generation, enjoy comparative ease, gather up
our feet in our beds, and die in peace; but our children will go
forth beggared from the homes of their fathers. Fishermen will
cast their nets where your proud commercial navy now rides at
anchor, and dry them upon the shore now covered with your bales
of merchandise. Sapped, circumvented, undermined, the institutions of your soil will be overthrown ; and, within five and twenty
years, the history of St. Domingo will be the record of Louisiana.
If dead men's bones can tremble, ours will move under the mut-
tered curses of sons and daughters, denouncing the blindness and
love of ease which have left them an inheritance of woe.

I have done my duty under as deep a sense of responsibility to
God and man as I have ever felt. Under a full conviction that
the salvation of the whole country is depending upon the action
of the South, I am impelled to deepen the sentiment of resistance
in the Southern mind, and to strengthen the current now flowing
toward a union of the South in defence of her chartered rights.
It is a duty which I shall not be recalled to repeat, for such awful
junctures do not occur twice in a century.

Bright and happy days are yet before us; and before another

political earthquake shall shake the continent, I hope to be " where the wicked cease from troubling and where the weary are at rest."

It only remains to say that, whatever be the fortunes of the South, I accept them for my own. Born upon her soil, of a father thus born before me—from an ancestry that occupied it while yet it was a part of England's possessions—she is, in every sense, my mother. I shall die upon her bosom; she shall know no peril but it is my peril—no conflict but it is my conflict—and no abyss of ruin into which I shall not share her fall. May the Lord God cover her head in this her day of battle !

Extract from the sermon of Rev. Henry J. Van Dyke, " Old School," of Brooklyn, New-York, referring to Dr. Thornwell, of South Carolina, and Dr. Palmer, of New Orleans, as being willing to secede from the Union :

" Whatever I may think of secession, as a remedy for the evils complained of, in my heart I do not blame them. My soul is knit to such men with the sympathy of Jonathan for David. Whatever be the result of this contest, the union between their hearts and mine, cemented by the word and Spirit of God, can never be dissolved. *Earth and hell cannot dissolve it.* Though my lot is cast in a colder clime, yet in the outgoings of that warm affection to which space is nothing, I will ever say, ' Entreat me not to leave thee, for your people shall be my people, and your God my God ;' and though we may be separated in body for a while by the dark gulf of political disunion, and by the absorbing strife for which every sound man at the North will soon be called upon to gird himself— *the long, long, rest of eternity, will afford abundant opportunity for the interchange of our mutual charities.*"

Extracts from Thanksgiving Sermon of Rev. Dr. Boardman, " Old School," of Philadelphia :

" But when you ask me, in the name of Christianity, to ' DENOUNCE THE SYSTEM OF SLAVERY as it exists at the South,' I tell you frankly, that, if I should stand up in this pulpit and do this thing, I should expect Christianity to denounce ME.

" There are, in the Southern States, (the fact is too weighty to be overlooked,) the same CHURCHES which exist at the North—with this difference, however : that a much greater proportion, probably, of their churches than of ours, are em - braced in the denominations styled ' Evangelical.' "

www.ingramcontent.com/pod-product-compliance
Lightning Source LLC
Chambersburg PA
CBHW020707260626
47157CB00008B/3183

* 9 7 8 3 3 3 7 3 6 1 7 0 9 *